All my best !

3/03/2022

The Purple Potion

SONIA OMOJOLA

The Purple Potion

Copyright © 2021: Sonia Omojola

Written by Sonia Omojola
www.soniaomojola.com

First Printed in United Kingdom, 2021

Published by Conscious Dreams Publishing
www.consciousdreamspublishing.com

Edited by Elise Abram

Typeset by Oksana Kosovan

ISBN: 978-1-913674-43-4

Dedication

This book is dedicated to my son, Zachariah,
whose birth gave me the inspiration
and passion to delve into the world of
The Purple Potion.

Contents

CHAPTER ONE The Treehouse 7

CHAPTER TWO The Baton 15

CHAPTER THREE The Call................................21

CHAPTER FOUR The Cave 33

CHAPTER FIVE The Chasm................................39

CHAPTER SIX The Herald 53

CHAPTER SEVEN The Village God 61

CHAPTER EIGHT The Mountain...........................73

CHAPTER NINE Leviathan.................................81

CHAPTER TEN Reunion...................................91

The Treehouse

There was nothing different about the day. The smell of the wet woodland infused the stillness of the air. Birds flocked together to search for their prey. The rivers glistened with rays of light, reflected from the sun. Along the trodden pathway, beyond the fields, lived an old man whose affection for his family ran deeper than the expanse of the ocean, and he spent many special hours nurturing his grandchildren in his humble abode.

⇥ ❋ ⇤

'I need you to listen well, son. I want to be sure that you will understand this time.'

The young boy's attention did not wane as he sat before his grandpa. His soft features frowned with a studious gaze. 'Okay, Grandpa,' was Jake's response.

The reception room in which they sat was filled with its usual aroma of old wooden furniture and used collectables. If it had not been for the finger trails on the windows etched in streaks of sunlight, Jake would never have known that the glorious, autumn sun was shining above the sea of golden-brown-leafed trees outside.

There was an unsteadiness in Grandpa's voice and a look of uncertainty on his face as he attempted to explain the story again. 'Okay, son, I will tell you.'

Grandpa dusted off his clothes and sat on the wooden chest, his elbow resting on his right leg. He studied Jake momentarily before proceeding. 'It was the legend…' Grandpa shook his head as if to wake himself up from drifting and let out a deep sigh, his eyes moving rapidly from side to side.

What was Grandpa thinking?

'I'm sorry son, I was just remembering some things.' He took another deep breath and paused as if to collect his thoughts.

He focused on his grandson. 'Legend has it that if one were to drink the Purple Potion during a blood moon, they would…' Grandpa paused. He sat upright in his mousy brown work clothes; their hems barely sewn.

Jake watched his grandpa's disposition. He was well-acquainted with the smell of the farm on his worn garments, which often rubbed off on his clothes during their journeys to harvest fresh vegetables for tea.

'They would what, Grandpa?'

'Live foreverrrr,' he said, his wise eyes widening.

Jake had heard him speak of the Purple Potion before, but he struggled to recall the details. He had been a small boy back then.

He laid down and listened intently. With his elbows on the floor, his hands on his cheeks, gazing into his grandpa's eyes, he said, 'Live forever? Really?'

Grandpa proceeded tentatively as if he were nervous that his grandson might not understand. 'Yes, my son. They will surely live forever, but you must understand that there are many trials to be seen by those brave enough to embark upon the search for it.'

Jake felt his eyes widen until he was sure they were the size of bronze Hemferplinian coins. 'We can search for it?"

'Yes, boy.'

Jake rolled onto his back and slid his hands beneath his head. He looked towards the old wooden ceiling and fathomed what could potentially be an extraordinary adventure.

'You see, my son, the potion calls out to those who are *chosen*. Only civilians with formidable characters are able to hold onto the emblem and live to speak of its secrets. No one – not one – knows of any who have tasted it and survived!'

Now, that was frightening. Jake turned quickly over and sat up to face his grandpa, who was seated upon the edge of the large antique chest. Silence froze their conversation momentarily as Jake's inexperienced thoughts attempted to piece together the logic, but there was nothing upon which to draw, for Jake had no knowledge to answer the complex feelings Grandpa's story aroused.

'But *why*, Grandpa?' was all Jake could think to say.

Grandpa's next words caused the hair on the back of his grandson's neck to stand on end. 'Many believe they have been called to find it, but sadly, only a few are *chosen*.'

There was a silence again as Grandpa Joe stared deeply into Jake's eyes. Why could Jake see a slight sadness beneath the surface of his light green eyes? Staring into those eyes was like peering into the lamp of his grandfather's soul. Jake shrugged off the thought, too anxious to know more.

Desperately confused, he asked, 'But how could one know, Grandpa?'

'Son, one cannot easily know.' Grandpa walked to the stained window, his back to Jake.

Why had this affected Grandpa so much?

'What's wrong, Grandpa?'

'Oh, nothing, son.' He wiped a tear from his eye, cleared his throat, and kneeled closely to the one he held so dear. Grandpa clasped his hands together in front of him and said, 'Only those who are true to themselves, those who have not been defiled by dark endeavours, can discern whether they are able to pass the test.'

What on earth were dark endeavours?

Grandpa paused again, interrupted as if a trail of thoughts were rushing through his mind with the speed of a forceful avalanche. He seemed to stop breathing for a brief second, and Jake thought he could hear his heart racing.

'Are you sure you're okay, Grandpa?'

Grandpa shrugged off his trance. 'Yes, boy.'

Then, like magic, optimism seemed to arise from within. 'But there's more.' There was a smile in his weary, watery eyes. 'The old man, full of age, one-hundred-and-seventeen years, is the only being left standing to tell the story behind the Purple Potion.'

Jake sensed his grandpa's joy. 'The old man?' he asked.

'Yes, son. When we find him, he will know!'

Jake stood to follow his grandpa as he hurried off. Trotting behind him, he questioned, 'Know what, Grandpa?'

'Know how to find the potion and live forever.' Grandpa paused. 'Come along – we must find him.'

Grandpa Joe rushed down into his old oak cottage's dusty basement with Jake following closely behind him. With a lantern in his hand, Grandpa shuffled through historical records he'd filed away. The adrenaline surge as he searched was infectious.

'What are you looking for, Grandpa?'

'His address, of course, son. His address!'

'But Grandpa, how did you get his address?' Jake's tone sounded innocent even to his own ears, and it seemed to strike to the core of Grandpa Joe's conscience.

As if trying to suppress the sense of guilt he felt from escaping, Grandpa confessed, 'Son, I am the keeper of the records. I really am supposed to keep them a secret, but child, we must find the old man. He is our only hope.'

→ ✳ ←

'Ring-a-ring o' roses, a pocket full of posies. A-tishoo! A-tishoo! We all fall down!'

'Stop playing that stupid game!' Jake shouted at his younger sister as she formed a circle with her friends.

Rosie looked disappointed, but her brother was not at all concerned. The two siblings were spending two weeks with their grandpa while their parents were away, trading cotton with the people of Zoar. It was a bright and mild day outside, with a gentle breeze of nutritious air. He could see the butterflies as they landed on an array of many-hued fragile petals, he could practically smell the flowers blossoming. The sound of crickets and birds enveloped the vicinity, making it sound like a buzzing beehive.

Jake moved through the ring of girls, ran out into the woods, and climbed into his childhood treehouse. He found it easier to focus up there, partly because it was the only place belonging to him where Rosie was not permitted to enter. Grandpa Joe had built it for his eighth birthday. Rosie had her own annexed hut, which she used as a playhouse from time to time when her friends would visit for tea.

He sat and pondered. Jake was about to turn from a twelve-year-old boy to a young man with an unquenchable resolve and sense of responsibility, and he continued to question where the old man could be. He used a piece of chalkstone to draw out a map of their small village on the wooden floor. The village of Reeva didn't have a large population, so finding the old man to whom Grandpa had alluded should be straightforward, he desperately hoped. He looked at the quintessential farming suburb mapped out before him and continued to reason with himself, questioning why he was so obsessed with finding the old man, and why he wanted to be the one to find the potion.

The weight of the answers to these questions was too much to comprehend. His determination to find the wise old man pressed down on him, and he focused on the task as might a skilled archer about to shoot a bullseye.

CHAPTER TWO

The Baton

'Grandpa – how's it going?' Jake said from the basement stairs, full of expectation and hope.

'The search is still going, son, come along.'

A day had come and gone, and Grandpa Joe was still shuffling through the records. The hope of finding the address seemed too dim. 'The old man would have registered at age sixteen, after all, that would have been over *one hundred years* ago,' he thought aloud.

The realisation of this seemed to permeate Grandpa's thoughts, making the task seem even more onerous. Just then, Grandpa's attitude brightened, as if a vivid memory had surfaced in his mind, as suddenly as if an invisible angelic guardian had dropped it there in passing. 'If he was a descendant of Godfrey-Jacob,' he thought aloud, 'his file would be in the seers' tray. How could I have forgotten that? Am I getting that old?'

'What's the seers' tray, Grandpa?'

'You see son, the Island of Hemferplin's archaic traditions had it that anyone and anything connected to the clan of seers were to be stringently documented due to problems with uprisings. Seers were known to cause controversial divisions due to information they possessed about the unknown.'

'The unknown?' Jake questioned.

'Yes, son, I will explain. Grab the ladder and climb!'

Jake pushed the ladder up against the dusty old wooden shelves and climbed as instructed. His pulse raced, and the palms of his hands were sweating, they had left wet marks on the rotting ladder rungs. The quest to find the potion had plagued him most of the night.

Grandpa moved towards the stack of files, breathing more deeply than usual, and pointed at the top shelf. With a croaky voice, he said, 'Reach for the silver tray, son.'

'But Grandpa, it's so dusty I can barely see anything.' Jake coughed as the dust particles latched onto the back of his throat, and he almost lost his balance.

'Careful, son!'

Jake steadied his feet, unfazed. He wiped the tray on the sixth shelf with the sleeve of his shirt to reveal its silver colouring. 'Yuk!' he said. "The Seers of Drakemore," he read aloud. 'Is this it?'

'Yes, son!' Joe retreated from the base of the ladder and reclined in the rocking chair behind him.

Jake quickly descended the ladder with the tray, which was full of documents, holding onto it tightly. He sat down on the grubby floor, placed the tray in front of him, and riffled through some letters. 'What's the old man's name, Grandpa?'

Joe looked at his grandson and leaned slightly forward, his right hand resting on his knee. He slowly withdrew his handkerchief from his left pocket and used it to wipe the sweat from his brow. Grandpa Joe caught his breath and said, 'Leviathan.'

'What? That's so weird!' Jake said. He felt his eyebrows raise, and he shook his head in disbelief. 'Who has a name like that?' He continued to shuffle through the historical records, his heart beating faster.

There were many papers with the heading, 'Importance Notice' written on them. Being curious, Jake read one. '"Dear Mr Jezrel, after numerous rumours about your involvement with the 'other world' and attempts to convey your apparent findings therein, we are hereby serving this notice. As a member of the seers' clan, you are forbidden to transmit messages from this apparent other world to the people of Drakemore or anywhere within the borders of Hemferplin. Any evidence which shall prove your involvement with the transmission of secret messages shall be treated with the utmost severity, resulting in punishment, or even expulsion, from the Hemferplinian Kingdom. This is to be treated as a formalised written notice.

In your service,

The Council"'

Jake took in a deep breath. 'Whoa,' he said. He folded the letter and put it back into the envelope. He gasped and read the back of the envelope: '"Leviathan J. Issachar, Hilltop Lakes, Drakemore, Hemferplin…"' 'Leviathan!' Jake exclaimed.

'Good job, son. Good job!'

Jake sat for a moment in silence, still stunned by the revelation contained in the letter to Mr Jezrel, considering the gravity of their quest.

While Jake was busy mulling over the implications of the letter, Grandpa Joe packed away the boxes they had emptied. Without warning, he grabbed his chest, and his body froze in excruciating pain.

'J-J-J-Jake – m-m-my heart!' he said, crying out for help. His fists clenched, the veins on his neck pulsated, and Grandpa collapsed to the ground, struggling to breathe as his face turned pale blue.

'Grandpa!' Jake rushed to his side and quickly undid the top buttons of his shirt to relieve the pressure from around his neck.

'It's y-y-your t-t-time, son. You m-m-must f-f-fight. Th-th-this ha-has a-a-all been about y-you.' With a final sigh, Grandpa Joe breathed his last breath. His head dropped onto Jake's shoulders, which now carried a load he was forced to bear.

Jake wept bitterly. 'This can't be!' he yelled.

'Grandpa, please come back!' he begged. 'I need you. Come back! Don't leave me, Grandpa! Whyyyy?!' he screamed.

Still holding Grandpa Joe in his arms, Jake continued to cry in deep grief. 'Please, Grandpa, come back. I need you!'

He sat there, hoping it was all a bad nightmare, and somehow, Grandpa Joe would open his eyes. Grandpa's last words weighed heavily on him, making him certain that he was at a crossroads, and his life was about to transition.

Never could he have imagined being thrust into a mission with such ferocity, but it was as though his soul was old enough to understand that the sequence of events playing out were no coincidence; Grandpa's final words had confirmed his inclination.

Jake began to have flashbacks of times when his grandpa had told him his life was significant, and that one day, he would be responsible for carrying out a great task. He hadn't understood it at the time, but he felt it had begun to make sense.

Rosie came into the basement, probably having heard Jake's screams.

'Don't look!' Jake cried, feeling a strong desire to protect her, but it was too late, and at only ten-years-old, Rosie witnessed her grandpa lying lifeless in her brother's arms.

She drew near them, tears rolling down her round cheeks. Her hands shook as she reached to embrace his soulless, weighty body. To Jake, Grandpa Joe looked as if he were asleep and at perfect peace with heaven.

Rosie sobbed gently. She asked, 'What happened?'

Jake looked down at his grandfather in contemplation, his eyes burning from hysterical weeping. He could no longer hide the feeling of fear and taste of bitterness he felt, yet his response seemed to draw from a place deeper than his shattered emotions, as if he had no power to restrict what he might say. 'He served his purpose, Rosie,' Jake told her. 'Now, I must serve mine.'

He closed Grandpa Joe's eyes, reached for the envelope with Leviathan's address, and climbed the basement stairs.

Rosie climbed the stairs, hurrying behind him.

CHAPTER THREE

The Call

Jake spent many days and long hours of solitude in his treehouse, distraught by the death of his grandpa, grappling with the enormity of the task tugging on his conscience.

Rosie would bring him bread and olives, but he refused to eat. He was too fearful, confused, and hurt.

A messenger had sent news to their parents by way of horse, and they returned from Zoar swiftly thereafter, extremely saddened and broken by the news. Although Grandpa Joe had been their paternal grandfather, he had treated their mother like his own child. Their father was so devastated he could barely speak for days. Their mother took care of the children, ensuring they had everything they needed to get by. There was, nevertheless, a huge vacuum in all their hearts.

Jane, his mother, came by periodically to check on her son. Jake knew she had grown increasingly concerned with how he was coping. He had lost weight and was looking lifeless and exhausted. Jake had been the closest to his grandpa, and his death had, evidently, affected him the most, and he refused to speak to anyone. The turmoil within him was like a raging sea.

The funeral took place as Grandpa Joe had wanted: a cremation with his ashes sprinkled over nearby Lake Precanto. Jake had many childhood memories of the lake, feeding bread to the ducks and bouncing pebbles across the water on the picnics on which their grandpa had taken them in the summer months. It was there that he would share stories of the other world with Jake, but he was too young at the time to remember most of them. Only now had he begun to recount them, but vaguely so.

Following the funeral, Jake returned to his treehouse, anxiously contemplating his grandpa's last words. He laid down, having grown weary with exhaustion, and fell into a deep sleep.

As he slept, an old man dressed in white with long grey hair, appeared to him and uttered, 'Jake, you have been called upon for a purpose. Do not neglect what has been entrusted to you. There are many who need your resolve and fortitude of character. They are waiting for you and are dependent upon your choices. Be of good courage and do not be afraid.' No sooner had the man finished than he disappeared in a thick mist.

Jake awoke, moving his hands across the floor beneath his unfed, weak body. He looked around to see the four walls of his carved-out, treasured, little treehouse.

But it was real, he reasoned. He had felt it. He struggled to shake off what he had experienced, but it had left an indelible impression on him.

Jake left the treehouse and ran into his sister's wooden hut, which was annexed to the cottage. 'Rosie, wake up.'

'What do you want?' she muttered.

'Wake up. We must go,' he whispered.

Rosie rubbed her squinted eyes and replied, 'Go where?'

'I will explain later.'

They grabbed lanterns to provide some much-needed light.

'Should I take food?' Rosie asked.

'Yes, take a little, but don't wake up Mumma and Pappa.'

Rosie hurried into the kitchen in the main cottage to pack some food. She met Jake on the porch, holding a large bag stuffed with bread and a wooden flask of water. Rosie looked at him and smiled cheekily.

Jake took his sister's hand and led the way, heading for their parents' horses. 'We'll take Mumma's,' Jake whispered.

They mounted Salsbury, their mother's chestnut Andalusian horse, and set off with Jake leading the way into the forest. Almost a mile into their journey, he felt the need to dismount Salsbury.

'Jake?'

'Yes, Rosie?'

'Where are you taking me?'

'Shh!'

'Why?'

Jake put his hand over Rosie's mouth and pulled her to one side. 'Shh,' he said again. 'Did you hear that?'

The horse galloped away.

Rosie did not speak. She only shook her head.

'Listen,' Jake said. 'There's a rustling sound in the bushes.'

Rosie pulled her brother's hand away from her mouth and whispered, 'It's probably the foxes. Jake, Salsbury's gone. Mumma will kill us.'

The sound became louder.

'Foxes don't cause the ground to tremble, Rosie.'

'No, you're right!'

The atmosphere grew eerier by the millisecond. Rosie clutched tightly onto her brother's arm as they looked up to see a dark shadow that eventually engulfed them.

The ground shook intensely. Before they had the chance to flee, an imposing, tall, rough-skinned, beast-like dark creature with piercing black eyes trampled out of the thick bushes.

Rosie screamed uncontrollably.

The creature roared as if it were a lion before asking, 'Who are you?'

Jake stood stationary as he looked directly into the beast's eyes and said, 'My name is Jake, and this is my sister, Rosie. We are from Reeva.' As soon as he'd said these words, he feared his boldness might trigger a negative reaction from the creature. When he'd left Reeva, he was prepared for a battle, but now he was gripped by the intimidation of not knowing how the journey might unfold.

'Bow down when spoken to,' the beast demanded.

Jake quickly bowed in complete subservience. He held Rosie – whose face was now immersed in the soil – close. There was a pause of complete silence as the beast examined them from a short distance away, sizing them up from head to toe.

'Enough! Follow me,' the creature insisted.

As the two-legged being led the way the ground before them opened into a set of descending stairs. It walked down the stairs with self-assurance and without a strand of welfare for the young seekers who had dutifully followed it and who were clutching each other's hands for security.

The atmosphere felt strange. The wind blew coolly, swirling the leaves about them like dancing lovers. It was as if the coolness of the air had dispelled every trace of Jake's fear.

Rosie lifted her head for the first time since their encounter with the beast. Her posture relaxed a bit, her face was no longer red from fright, and her pink cheeks showed through the streaks of dirt.

A strength came over Jake, giving him a sense of encouragement.

The beast glanced behind him, seemingly aware of the transformation that had taken place within the siblings. As they descended the stairs, the being explained himself. 'I didn't mean to frighten you,' it said. 'I just needed to be sure of who you were.'

Jake nodded, and Rosie smiled half-heartedly. They looked at each other in amazement, as the creature's eyes had turned a light brown, and the sound of his voice had become more human-like, losing its animalistic growl.

The steps were steep, and they continued their descent as if on a precarious mountain trail. On either side of them were walls mounted with crowns and shields in various metals, some of them shinier than others. The smell of incense infused the air – lavender, myrrh, rose, and dew – becoming stronger the deeper they went. A mist glided faintly through the air before them like a whistling wind.

This was the other world, Jake realised.

The beast looked back as if he had heard Jake's thoughts and nodded to confirm his observation.

Smiling with excitement, Rosie looked at her brother and whispered, 'I heard your thoughts, too.'

'Nothing is hidden in the other world,' the beast explained. 'All things are seen, and all things are known.'

So, there *was* another world.

'Yes, but only those with – '

'Formidable character may enter.' Jake felt his cheeks colour after he'd finished the beast's sentence. Boy and beast smiled at each other.

'You've learned well, child.'

'Beast?' Rosie queried.

The beast looked back through the corner of its eye and said, 'You can call me Erwin.' With that, his stature slowly decreased to the size of a human, just under six-feet tall. Its rough skin shed from its back like a moulting snake to reveal clothing. The transformation felt natural to the siblings observing it, yet surreal. It was as if they had always known him as a person and not a beast.

Rosie responded to Erwin's change with a huge smile, revealing her beautiful white, levelled teeth and round freckled cheeks.

'Erwin?'

'Yes, Rosie Jane?'

Rosie turned to her brother and giggled, probably because Erwin had known her middle name. 'Where are you from?' she asked.

'The other world, of course.'

'No, I mean, where are you *originally* from?'

The expression on Erwin's face seemed to indicate that he knew he wasn't dealing with an ordinary ten-year-old. 'I see this is why your brother chose you to come with him,' Erwin told her. 'Brains like yours are needed for such a cumbersome task.'

Did he know? Jake wondered.

Erwin looked at Jake, who instinctively avoided eye contact. 'She has the mind of my mother,' Jake muttered.

Rosie stopped, lifted her head, threw back her shoulders, and said, 'My mother trades cotton with foreigners, and one day, I'm going to be as strong and successful as she is.'

Erwin paused then said, 'Indeed,' and continued descending the stairs with the siblings following closely behind him. The end of the staircase was now in sight.

'So…where *are* you from, Erwin?' Jake asked.

'Well, if you must know, I'm from a small village called Drakemore.' Erwin was fully human by then. Jake tried to figure out when his metamorphosis had ended.

'We were expelled due to the uprisings when we warned our people about the other world. We became a threat to Chief Warrior and Leader of the Council Sebastian every time we convinced a local that the unseen was real. Because of their newfound hope, people ceased celestial worship and refrained from offering their livelihood to gain a place in the afterlife with the unknown gods. They called those people seers.'

Chills went down Jake's spine. He could hardly believe what he was hearing. 'How did you survive?' Jake asked.

'We were chased to the edge of Hemferplin, and the only way forward for us was by way of the Illunaus Waters. We had heard stories from our forefathers that no one had ever crossed the Illunaus and lived to talk about it.'

'Yes,' Jake recalled. 'My grandpa told me there were sea spirits there.'

'Yes, he was right. Little did we know that the other world could be accessed from anywhere. We jumped, all eleven of us. The moment we cried out, we were safe. The guardians of the other world accepted our souls and opened the pathway, which we have had access to ever since. It was as if a pillar of smoke had enveloped us as we fell through the air from the top of the cliff. It all happened so quickly, as fast as the blink of an eye.'

Jake listened, absorbing each word.

'But our deepest regret was leaving Leviathan – they wouldn't let him go. We tried to take him with us, but Sebastian's soldiers chained him to a tree in the centre of the village until we had gone. They wanted to ensure they would still have contact with the other world by using his powers if they needed safety from foreign invaders. They tried to harm us to keep us quiet on many occasions, but they were always unsuccessful. By this, they knew we carried a protection they coveted.'

Rosie took a few steps down, touched Erwin's arm and asked, 'Erwin, are you okay?'

They all stopped as he spoke, standing just a couple steps from the bottom of the trail. 'Leviathan is my eldest brother. I miss him so dearly. Whilst he was chained to the tree, many people mocked and spat on him. They hurled insults, shouting, "If you know hidden secrets, tell us: who spat on you?"'

Erwin looked at Jake as if he could see every secret he possessed and said, 'When I caught news of your quest to find him, I knew I had to help.'

29

Jake was surprised by what he was hearing and asked, 'Who told you I was looking for Leviathan?'

'You are a part of us, Jake. Your Grandpa Joe was a very special person. His role as the keeper of records was given to him because he was a trusted hero. He possessed great power but never wanted to associate himself with the seers because of the love he had for his family and out of fear for your safety, he left us to live in Reeva. You were all so very dear to him.

'The potion had called to him, but he refused to drink it, saying he was not ready. Instead, he thought that one day, a greater vessel would arise, and he would ensure he was prepared for the battle to find it. He chose to trade his power for you.'

Tears of understanding streamed down Jake's face. 'He sacrificed himself for *me*,' he cried. 'He gave up his powers to be with me and protect me.'

'Jake, please don't cry.' Rosie wiped the tears from her brother's eyes and squeezed his body tightly. 'Grandpa Joe is watching out for us, okay?'

No sooner had she released him from the hug than she slipped and fell to the ground. 'Ouch!' she said, having twisted her foot on the wet, uneven, final stony steps beneath her.

'Rosie, are you okay?' Jake quickly wiped his eyes and kneeled at the bottom of the steps to help her. He looked around and perceived he was somewhere different. Forest trees surrounded them, but he was more focused on his sister, and he examined Rosie's ankle.

Erwin kneeled swiftly to offer some help, too.

'It really hurts,' Rosie said, staring at her ankle, which was red and swollen.

Erwin rushed out into the open green forest, pulled a large green leaf from the tree hanging above him, and wrapped it around her swollen ankle.

Seconds later, Rosie said, 'Oh, my, Erwin – I can move my ankle. The pain has gone. I feel completely fine. Thank you!' Rosie stood and jumped into the air, laughing as she tested the strength of her ankle. 'It feels even better than before,' she shouted as she spun around with excitement that seemed to flow through her like electricity.

There was something special about the place in which they now stood. They had reached the end of the staircase and were surrounded by large trees and wet woodland, but it looked more like a beautiful jungle. The birds sang as they flew high above the tall, earthy-smelling stalks. The light from the bright blue, cloudless sky shone gracefully upon them, peeking out through the branches.

Erwin smiled and said, 'We have arrived.'

CHAPTER FOUR

The Cave

'Thomas, my brother, please take the children to the Dark Closet and dress them for battle!'

'Certainly, Erwin,' responded a tall senior-looking relative.

Rosie smiled at her brother as she swung her arms in excitement above the hem of her mustard yellow, corduroy dress. Jake smiled back, scaling his surroundings.

They had entered a large, cave-like home. Birds flew around freely inside, and tree trunks were used as pillars to support the infrastructure. There was a small stream on either side of a grey-bricked pathway, which led to the sleeping chambers. On one of the doors ahead of them was written, 'HKGX DXXY' in the ancient dialect of Hemferplinese, which translated to 'Dark Closet' – Jake's grandpa had taught him the language from the age of six.

'Wow,' Rosie said.

While the others approached the Dark Closet, Rosie paused in front of a large wooden door about eight-feet tall, wedged slightly open. Her curiosity seemed to have got the best of her, and she peeked her head around the door, trying to open it further. Her gasps caught Jake's attention, and he watched as her eyes widened, and she raised her eyebrows. When a muscular panther paced the floor inside the room circling the large four-poster bed, Jake felt his eyebrows raise, too.

Thomas looked over his shoulder, pulled Rosie away, and hurried to close the door, locking it with a long, rusty, ancient-style key.

Thomas's demeanour was one of compliance. It was as if he were doing everything under orders, though his submission did not appear forced or controlled. There was a genuine happiness about him as he went about fulfilling his duties.

'That is your master, Erwin's, chamber,' Thomas informed Rosie.

'Oh,' she responded slowly. 'I'm sorry. I was just – '

'It's okay,' Thomas interrupted. 'I see that your inquisitiveness is innocent. I just didn't want to frighten you.'

Thomas looked back across the bridge and whistled as two lions seemed to appear from nowhere, crossed their paths, and trod towards them until there was one standing on either side of Jake and Rosie.

'Who are these?' Rosie asked, stroking both lions. 'They seem rather friendly for lions.'

'They will become your closest acquaintances. The panther you saw in your master's chamber has been through many wars. He has protected your master since he was a small boy, but the two only met each other when Erwin was expelled from Hemferplin. Only then did he feel the most deserted, and the need to be physically secure was too intense for him to bear. When the panther revealed his presence, it brought great comfort to Erwin, and the two have been inseparable since. His protective powers have kept many dark forces away from Erwin, and indeed, from the other world. He stands as the chief keeper and king of the other world, and your master, Erwin, is the general.'

Jake listened intently as Rosie told her lion her full name, favourite food, and about Grandpa Joe. 'We have a lot more talking to do,' she said as the lion rubbed its body against hers.

Jake looked at his sister and smiled warmly. Rosie was confident and forthright. She had all the characteristics of their mother, which brought him much joy.

'Now, come along,' Thomas said. 'You two must get dressed. The lions will be waiting when you return.'

→ ❊ ←

Thomas opened the door to the Dark Closet and led the way up some concrete stairs. The walls there were embedded with various armoury: shields and swords and bows and arrows. Jake touched them as he walked past.

Thomas looked back at him and smiled.

As if Jake had read his thoughts, he asked, 'Which armour was his?'

Thomas – who had a calming look on his face – looked at Jake again. His eyes were light grey and looked as if they hid the stories of many adventures. Jake sensed a fatherly feel to his presence, and he gravitated towards it.

'He was a stout young man, so his helmet was larger than usual. You see the round, dim-coloured one above the lantern?'

'Yes, I see it.'

It was quite high up, so Thomas offered to lift Jake up to touch it. 'Here you go – have a feel.'

Jake stepped into the crook Thomas made with his lowered hands and reached up to touch the helmet. He was silent as he stepped back down, absorbed in the moment and the sense of pride he felt from the privilege he had just experienced.

'That was his. Randolph was his name,' Thomas continued. 'He had no friends and was a real loner. He was also a grandchild on the seers' lineage. The trouble was that he had lost his sight from the sand dust in a storm he encountered on his way back to the other side, so we sent him back to his family to recover, and we stripped him of his armour.'

'The two of you must stay intact. You need to be sharp and ready for any plot or scheme from the unseen forces.'

Rosie reached out for Jake's hand and squeezed it tightly.

They walked up the final steps. The smell of burnt metal filled the air, and the temperature increased to above fifty degrees Celsius, but strangely, the heat did not harm them.

There, in the room lit by the fire from the furnace, was a short man, his face covered with a mask and wearing protective clothing as he used a set of long tongs to remove molded armoury from the blaze.

'It's all prepared, sir,' the man said. 'Just getting the young girl's helmet ready. Size four, right?'

'That's correct, Basel,' Thomas replied.

'Their sheepskin capes are hanging and clean, and their leather sandals have fresh buckles and soles. Their armour should be cooled off by now and is fully shined. I've been working on them since noon, sir.'

'Oh, thank you, Basel!' Rosie exclaimed.

Basel turned to look at Rosie, who was almost his size, grinned, and said, 'You are welcome.'

Thomas looked at her and grinned, too.

Jake's mouth opened as he looked in awe at the fine works of armour that had been made for the two of them.

CHAPTER FIVE

The Chasm

The siblings had spent a few hours exploring the grand home before Thomas interrupted them. 'Time to leave now,' he said. 'Your satchels are packed, and your lions are on their way from being groomed and fed, which will sustain them until you reach the other side. They will meet you at the gate.'

'Which gate?' Jake and Rosie asked in unison.

Thomas looked at Erwin as if he were unprepared to give an explanation.

'You cannot leave the way you entered,' Erwin answered. 'That pathway is not known to anyone except the seers. When you leave, you will be thrust into a chasm, the world between Hemferplin and the other world. It is there that battles will be fought before the ultimate crossover.'

'You must understand that a mature seer cannot pass there, for, after the expulsion, there was a demarcation placed around us, which means we cannot fully return. The chief keeper of other world keeps and protects us, which is why we have been unable to rescue Leviathan — we cannot breach the injunction placed upon us.'

'If I said I wasn't scared, I'd be lying,' Jake said.

'Me, too,' Rosie added.

'Come with me. I want to show you both something.' Erwin led them to a long stretch of a tall, black, metal fence, situated at the end of a small pathway to the rear of the cave. Thomas followed quietly behind them. There, they saw the lions, prostrate and waiting patiently for the young siblings.

'You see that house?' Erwin motioned for Jake to look through a large, rectangular, ancient-looking wooden frame built into the metal fence. It was decorated with words in the ancient dialect of Hemferplinese.

Jake saw an old house in the distance, sitting upon a mountain beyond an array of woodland. A single window was lit from the inside by a yellow light. 'Yes, I see it,' Jake responded.

Rosie was occupied stroking her lion, which seemed to have become as familiar with her as if they had known each other for many years.

'Inside that chamber is where they are keeping Leviathan.'

Rosie stopped what she was doing and turned her head. '*What?* Let me see! Are you saying that he's that close?'

'Yet so far,' Jake muttered. He knew that what he was seeing was through the view of the Magitheum. Grandpa Joe had told him about it – the lens of purity. Through it, he could see everything from the other world. Through the pure Magitheum, you could see anything you wanted.

Seeing where Leviathan was being kept gave Jake great determination to go. 'Wait – before we go, can we please see our parents?' Jake requested without thinking about what he had asked.

'Yes, sure,' Erwin responded, 'but please, be prepared for what you might see. People are used to only knowing a fraction of reality on the other side of the other world, but here, *nothing* is hidden.'

Jake felt these words hit the deepest part of his heart like a dagger sharp enough to pierce flesh easily. He sat down, placed his head in his cupped hands, and shook his head as if to shake off anxiety. The reality of their quest began to play upon his mind, and he suddenly realised how far they had travelled without their beloved parents. He felt his hands gently shake, and his heart skipped its usual beats. Up until that point, he had been excited about their adventure. He lifted his head up and said, 'No, I don't think it would be a good idea to see them, I need to remain focused.'

'Jake, please – let's just see what they are doing,' Rosie pleaded.

'I'm scared, Rosie. I think seeing them will be too much for me!' He walked off and sat on a small rock a short distance from the others. His lion followed closely behind him.

With tears streaming down his face, Jake cried, 'I can't bear to see my parents, lion. I thought I wanted to, but I just *can't.*'

His new companion responded with a gentle growl, and Jake held his head near the animal's mane.

'I miss them so much and want to be near to them. I also want them to see this beautiful world and be all right with us not being with them right now. I want them to know that we are fine, but my mother, she will be so worried, especially about Rosie, and my father will be disappointed that we left without letting them know where we were going.' He wiped his eyes.

'But now, going back to get Leviathan – it's just the craziest adventure, and I have mixed emotions about it; I'm excited, scared, *and* uncertain.

'Lion, I need you to stay close to me. I need you by my side. I need you to watch out for Rosie and me. Promise you will.'

The lion rubbed his body against Jake's legs in response.

'I would love to see my parents, Erwin.' Jake overheard his sister say excitedly.

Jake looked over his shoulder and saw Rosie climb up on a ledge to look through the Magitheum.

'Oh, look – I can see my mother in my room. She's tidying up my scarves and placing them in my wooden box. Oh no, she's crying, Erwin.' Rosie looked surprised by the depth of her mother's pain. 'There's our father, too, near Grandpa Joe's cottage on the Hilltop of Pikascia, chopping wood for the fire. He looks so anxious, Erwin.'

Rosie sat down, looking stunned by what she had seen. 'Thank you, Erwin.'

Jake came over with his lion. 'We are ready,' he said.

'I saw them, Jake. I think you should look, even if it's just for a few seconds.'

'Okay. I'll look.' He walked towards the fence, grasped the bars in his hands, bowed his head, and looked slowly through the Magitheum, squinting his eyes. He gradually opened his eyelids until he had a full view of the look on his father's face as he chopped the wood. He also saw the distraught look in his mother's eyes.

'I have seen more than enough. Send me out. This quest is not in vain! Our parents must see that the search to find the Purple Potion is not just for me, but it is for them, also. Grandpa did not sacrifice himself just for me but for our entire family, my mum, dad, sister, and others, too.'

He said that remembering the dream he had in his treehouse had spurred him to leave Reeva when the old man told him that many were relying on his choices.

Jake kneeled and stroked his lion while he looked out beyond the fence, giving him a view of the thick mist and hilltops in the far distance. It looked like a land of nothingness, which made Jake wonder where all the battles would take place.

The siblings hugged each other and held hands.

'Jake, you will need this.' Thomas handed him a glass bottle with a scroll inside.

'These are your directions,' Erwin confirmed.

'Thank you.' Jake dug into his pocket, pulled out a crumpled piece of paper, and showed Erwin its contents. 'I have this.'

Erwin took it from him and read the details of Leviathan's address. 'That was our family's home before the expulsion,' he told Jake. 'You won't be needing that anymore. Leviathan is no longer there.'

'Okay. Now, remember to keep your armour on at all times – you just do not know when you are going to need it.'

Jake placed the scroll into his satchel and nodded. He and Rosie stood in front of the gate with their lions, posed like soldiers ready for war, and the gate opened on its own accord. A strong wind encompassed them, sweeping the pair into the dim, foggy atmosphere. Their lions seemed to appear beneath them, and Jake and Rosie landed on their backs as they flew through the air.

'Be bold!' Erwin shouted, his voice echoing in the wind.

A tenacity overtook them, aided by Erwin's words which penetrated to the very core of their being. They continued riding their lions through the wind, though they were barely able to see where they were going.

'Where are our weapons?' Jake asked once he realised the shiny amour they had been wearing had disappeared. All that remained were their satchels, sheepskin capes, and leather sandals.

Rosie had been puffing from the speed of their flight. She caught her breath and shouted back, 'I don't know!' Rosie took a deep breath. 'Ride, lion, ride!' she said, instructing her lion to push through the wind.

The lions followed her instructions and rode through the ferocious winds, but when the lions began to growl, the siblings knew something was wrong. Their suspicions were confirmed when the lions separated.

'Wait!' Jake shouted. 'Where are you going, lion? Take me back to my sister!'

A huge black eagle with light yellow eyes flapped its long, majestic wings and went after Jake. Its beak went straight for his satchel.

'Hey, leave my satchel alone!' Jake shouted, fighting off the eagle by waving his arms. As soon as the words had left his mouth, a shiny, long, heavy silver sword fell from the sky and right into his right hand.

Jake looked directly into the eagle's eyes. 'Die!' he screamed as he thrust the sword into the black bird's chest. Jake looked down at the eagle as it fell into the whirlwind, screeching after it had lost its ability to fly and was taken up by the storm.

'Wow, that was close! Jake said.

The lions redirected back towards each other.

'Not bad.' Rosie smiled and high-fived her brother.

The lions glanced at each other like team players who had dodged and overcame their opponents.

Their direction changed again, and the lions began a speedy descent.

'Whoaaaa!' they both cried.

'This is so much fun!' Rosie shouted.

Within seconds, they had landed on the dusty ground, surrounded by a large scattering of boulders. They both dismounted their lions.

'Who taught you to fight like that, Jake?' Rosie asked.

Unsure of what to say, Jake shrugged his shoulders. 'It came naturally, I guess.'

'Umm…where's your sword?' Rosie asked, having assessed her brother's person.

Jake shrugged. 'I just had it.'

Then, a huge flying green beetle circled Jake's head. Before he could even think, a swatter appeared in his left hand. 'Get away!' he shouted. He jumped into the air and knocked the deadly insect to the ground. He looked at his hand, but the swatter had vanished. It was then Jake understood that their weapons would appear only when needed.

'I guess the amour was a little heavy.' Rosie giggled.

'Yes, it was.' Jake said as he examined his hands. 'I just hope I can get used to this way of navigating.' He felt his face frown as he scouted their surroundings. 'Hmm…*Now*, where are we?' Jake questioned. The place was desolate, and he could find no signs of human life in such dry and lifeless pastures.

The lions appeared to be waiting by their sides for instructions on their next course of action.

'I'd better make sure I hold onto this.' Jake took the glass bottle out of his satchel, removed the scroll, and searched for directions. The details on the map were quite small, but he was pleased to see that Thomas had placed a magnifying glass in his satchel.

'He's a good man,' Jake said to himself, referring to Thomas, whom he deemed a faithful friend.

'Can you see anything?' Rosie asked.

After studying the sketches on the scroll, he said, 'It's no use, Rosie – the map doesn't have the chasm on it.' Jake placed the scroll back into his satchel.

'So, what do we do now?'

'I think it's best for us to walk up north in the direction away from where we came.'

'Makes sense to me,' Rosie agreed.

They began to walk northwards, and the lions followed. Jake was unsure of where they were heading.

Rosie said, 'Jake, look – can you see that dark cloud? It looks like it's moving towards us.'

Jake saw a black shadow in the far distance, but its form was difficult to decipher. Its pace was quick, and there was a loud screeching sound. Jake could see that it was moving towards them.

'Jake, look – I can see more!'

The shadow began to multiply. Jake studied the bizarre apparition. It didn't take long before the sound of many creatures filled the sky. They continued to increase in number, looking like teeming bees escaping from their hive.

'Bats!' Jake shouted. 'Run!' Jake's heart pounded heavily inside his chest. They ran so fast, the dust beneath their feet arose like smoke from the ground. With great skill, they jumped onto their lions and rode valiantly through the rocky terrain.

Fear filled Jake's heart as the bats chased them relentlessly. They were soon surrounded and outnumbered. The colony was far too powerful and great in number, and the siblings knew there was no escape.

'There's so many of them!' Rosie cried with a look of desperation.

The lions stopped and began walking in circles, roaring as they strode.

With a sense of powerlessness, Jake looked at his sister and asked, 'What shall I do?'

The bats flew closely above their heads, screeching so loud, Jake could hardly think.

'I don't know why,' Rosie said, 'but I feel as if you should throw your shield at them!'

'What shield?'

Jake hadn't realised he was holding a shield in his hand. He looked down at it and hesitated before throwing it with all his might. It spun into the midst of the colony, emitting a sound like a gushing wave, confusing the bats who lost their direction. Some of them fell to the ground, dying instantly, while others scattered in fear.

'It worked!' Jake exclaimed. 'Well done, Rosie!' Jake wiped the sweat from his brow with his outer garments and high-fived his sister.

'I'm tired, Jake.' Rosie had become wearisome as they continued north, and she seemed to be falling slowly asleep.

Jake reached for a rope in his satchel and tied her securely to her lion's back.

By then, they had been travelling for three days straight. It was cold, and they all needed some rest. Since the bat attack, their journey had been easy, and Jake decided that they were in an ideal place to seek out shelter.

The lions continued to carry the siblings. Jake felt a rattle in his satchel. At first, he ignored it, thinking it was his tired imagination, but then, he felt it again, stronger this time. Unable to dismiss the vibration, he stopped and opened his bag. He felt his eyebrows raise, and he rubbed his eyes.

The glass bottle was rattling around inside the satchel unaided, and the scroll inside was illuminated. Jake scurried off his lion and unrolled the ancient map on the muddy ground. Green trees populated what seemed to be the area on the map that marked where they had stopped.

It was as if the place they had stopped was being created on the map in real-time.

The light coming from it was so bright, it shone into Jake's face as he peered into the living, breathing world before him.

They had moved from a dry, lifeless territory to a place of green, full of trees, bushes, and vitality without having realised it. Jake was relieved for he wished to see a good-willed comrade to assist with their quest, and he felt the map provided some much-needed reassurance. He had begun to feel quite lonely on their journey, mostly because he did not know where it would lead.

There was life all around them, which was good. It was very good.

Jake looked around. There was a lake nearby, and he walked towards it to fill his flask with some water and drink. It was refreshing and much-needed, for his mouth had become as dry as a scorched desert.

He looked back over at the others, felt a cool breeze on his arms, and realised that the night was drawing near. Jake went back to their resting spot and continued to scale the map, which had lost its illumination. Soon, he, too, started to feel tired and exhausted.

The lions were fast asleep. The two of them and Rosie were lying together, so he released his sister from the rope and covered her with two large leaves taken from a nearby bush.

The trees surrounding them lowered their branches to form an enclosure above their heads in the shape of a small hut. It felt comforting, as though every tree had a mind of its own, and they were nurturing them. The temperature increased, and Jake began to warm as the abundance of leaves on the branches blocked out the chill.

They all slept that night, protected, and covered.

⤙⁂⤚

'Jake?' called the old man.

'Yes, sir?'

'You've done well to have come this far. Many were unable to fight in the same manner that you fought the eagle and the colony of bats. You've heeded well.'

'Heeded what, sir?'

'Your inner-powers. Every choice you have made has been a consequence of your inner-compass.'

'What's an inner-compass?'

'It's what guides your decisions. You've matured since last we spoke, and it's an honour to watch your progress.'

Jake sat still in front of the old man, listening intently. 'Where can I find you?'

'Your inner-compass will lead you to where you should go.'

'Thank you, Leviathan.'

Jake awoke. Hold on, he thought. The old man in his dream had been Leviathan.

It was the middle of the night, and the others were still sleeping, and Jake decided it would be best to set out in the morning.

CHAPTER SIX

The Herald

Rosie peered through a hole in their hut of branches and leaves, inviting a ray of sunlight into their incubated shelter. She giggled as she watched a squirrel manoeuvring about with a hazelnut in its paws. The lions were still lying down, keeping watch of their surroundings.

Jake sat up and watched his sister being entertained. He rubbed his eyes and asked, 'What time is it?'

Still peering through the hole, Rosie replied, 'It's time we eat some breakfast.' She pulled the branches farther apart and gestured for her brother to join her. The sunlight shone directly into his eyes as he moved towards the hole, and he welcomed its warmth.

'Now, look,' Rosie said. 'See that squirrel? He knows exactly where to go to get more of where *that* came from. Let's follow him and find them. We can roast hazelnuts for breakfast.'

Jake rubbed his eyes again, and he looked at the squirrel. 'Okay,' Jake said, complying with his sister's idea. 'I'll start the fire, and you can gather the hazelnuts.'

Rosie set out with her lion to gather some food for breakfast. Jake saw her spot three squirrels while walking, congregating under a nearby tree, and she followed them in search of the hazelnuts, her lion striding closely behind her. Rosie laughed at the manner in which the squirrels appeared to be speaking to each other, wobbling their little heads as they did, and she crouched and stroked one of their tails before they ran off.

'Wow, you lit that fire quickly!" Rosie said when she came back from gathering the nuts.

'It's not lit yet. I'm still rubbing the sticks,' Jake replied.

Rosie looked and saw this was true. 'Then, why can I smell smoke?' She covered her nostrils and moved closer to where her brother was sitting and rubbing the sticks.

'Can you smell that?' Rosie asked.

Before he could answer, the lions growled. Jake stood up and looked at them, trying to ascertain why they felt so uneasy. 'There, there, lions,' he said to placate them as he continued to analyse what they might be trying to communicate.

The lions stared towards where the squirrels had congregated.

Jake stepped forward and confirmed, 'Hmm…Yes, I *can* smell smoke.'

The temperature around them began to heat rapidly, and a dark shadow glided above them like a cloak. There was a strange, lingering presence about them. A foul smell infused the air, almost strong enough to taste. Leaves and wooden sticks in the vicinity crackled and popped.

Rosie looked down and said, 'Jake, can you feel the ground beneath us? It's heating up!'

Fire burst through the soil without warning, gushing forth with high velocity like lava from a volcano, encircling them, leaping around them as if executing a tribal dance.

Rosie cried hysterically, 'Jake, do something!'

Jake's lion stood up, balanced on its two hind legs, and pounced on Jake's chest, causing him to fall backwards. It released a mighty roar as it stood over him.

'Okay,' Jake said, 'okay…you want me to do something, but what?'

There were no weapons or armour for him to use to escape the flames, and nothing came to Jake's assistance. 'Where are you now, Erwin? Where are you now, Leviathan?'

'Jake!' Rosie cried.

'Okay…okay…I'm thinking.' Jake looked rapidly from side to side.

'Jake, we're burning up!' Rosie cried.

Jake stood and looked at his sister and the lions with fear and resolve. 'My inner-compass will guide me. We are trapped, and the only way out for us is to run through the fire,' he shouted above the crackle of the flames.

'Jake, are you crazy? We can't run through the fire. We will all die!'

'Rosie, you have to trust me. This is what we must do. Mount your lion, Rosie!'

Rosie climbed onto her lion, trembling like a leaf.

Jake followed suit, jumping onto his lion. 'Lions, are you ready?' Jake asked.

They growled in agreement and stood on their hind legs.

'I will count to three: one…two…three!'

The lions roared their loudest since they had met the siblings and jumped into the blaze. The roars turned to screams as they rode fearlessly into the furnace. It felt like forever, but they landed on the other side within fifteen seconds, mercifully unscathed by the flames.

The siblings dismounted their lions and ran quickly towards each other. They sobbed together as Jake held his sister against his chest.

Rosie looked up into her brother's eyes and whispered, 'We made it.' She squeezed him tightly, kneeled, and hugged her lion. With tears in her eyes, she thanked her lion and declared, 'From now on, I'm going to call you Rex.'

Jake caressed his lion's head and said, 'And you will be called Dux.'

The siblings looked around. There were houses in the distance with cows grazing on acres of green pastures. The air smelled as fresh as water from a spring. They looked behind them to find that they were surrounded by farmland, and the forest had disappeared.

Jake smiled heartily for the first time since his grandpa had died and whispered, 'We've crossed over.'

'Residents of Drakemore – there are three days before the blood moon will cause our small village to be soused in darkness. Three days!' the messenger heralded.

Jake and Rosie caught their breaths after having run for cover behind a large rock. 'That was so close,' she whispered. 'You seemed to know what he was talking about. I saw it in your eyes. What *is* the blood moon, Jake?'

'It's the legend Grandpa told me about. We must find Leviathan before it happens. The potion must only be drunk during the blood moon,' Jake whispered back.

'And then what? You die?'

'No, I will live forever.'

Rosie turned her head, raised her eyebrows, and responded, 'This is a selfish mission if it's all about you living forever.'

'It's not! Grandpa Joe said the potion called out to the chosen ones, and Leviathan came to me that night while I was asleep to tell me there were people depending on me, Rosie. I don't know why – I'm not exactly special, am I? I just know I need to find it. Everything within me says I do. The old man, Leviathan, will explain it all when we rescue him. He's the only one who fully understands, Rosie.'

Rosie sat, clutching her knees together. It was too late to go back, and Jake knew she didn't want to. He also knew that she believed every word. 'So, where do we go from here, then?' she asked. 'This village looks so different from where we came from, and the people are far from approachable. I thought that messenger would pin us up by the ears if he saw us.'

The two siblings were all alone. Their lions had bid them farewell once they'd reached the village entrance, seeming to have disappeared into thin air. Their role as the children's physical guardians was mostly just until they had crossed over the chasm. They were not permitted to be seen by people on the other side, able only to rush to their assistance if the children were in significant danger. Jake still felt their presence from time to time. Rosie told him that she was especially aware of their presence – she had what Jake described as an ability to feel the unseen like the child of a goddess.

Jake pulled the scroll from his satchel, held it up in the air, and pointed at a bird-like symbol on it. He said, 'According to this, we need to head eastward towards the statue of Hermes, their village god.'

'Well, let's go!' Rosie said.

'Wait – I think we should wait to leave until the sun goes down. We are new to this area, and I don't want us to attract unnecessary attention, which could delay our mission. We only have three days to find Leviathan, and we need to be careful, so we aren't held up by anyone or anything. It's warm enough; let's rest here for a couple of hours. We still have some food in our satchels – let's eat and regain some strength.'

'I suppose you're right.'

Rosie laid her sheepskin cape on the floor next to Jake, and he did the same. They rested for a couple of hours on the foreign ground, watching Drakemore's mysterious sun go down.

'Rosie?'

'Yes, Jake. I'm all ears.'

'How do you feel about this mission? Do you think we'll be successful?'

'To be honest, I'm feeling pretty hungry right now.' Rosie giggled as she passed Jake some of the bread she had taken when leaving Reeva along with a few raw hazelnuts from the forest.

They ate heartily and drank some of the water Jake had taken from the river.

After he had finished eating the bread, Jake said, 'Really, though, Rosie – tell me how you feel.'

'Jake, when we were stuck in the blaze, you said that your inner-compass would guide you, and you were right. I feel like you must trust the same compass that got us out of danger in the chasm. It hasn't failed us so far.'

Jake smiled, then rubbed the crown of his sister's head and whispered, 'That's why I love you. Let's go now.'

CHAPTER SEVEN

The Village God

Darkness settled over the sky as they headed eastward towards the statue of Hermes, but there was something unsettling about the atmosphere as they approached the village god's vicinity. The locals appeared lifeless, as if their souls had been stripped from their inner-beings, and all that remained were the shells of their bodies. The peoples' clothes were in tatters, as if they were poor or homeless, which seemed strange for a working precinct such as theirs. It would seem completely normal if whatever it was had affected the odd person or even two or three of the people they passed, but the entire village looked dire and barren.

'I've never seen anything like it,' Rosie exclaimed.

'Me neither, Rosie.'

They walked through the open streets as they spoke, but it appeared as though the people had not noticed their existence. Rosie approached a young girl holding a bowl of water on her head and dared to touch her arm gently.

'Greetings,' she said. 'We are looking for a man called Leviathan.'

There was no response. The girl walked on by without even the flicker of an eyelid, as if she had not even seen or heard Rosie speaking to her.

Rosie went on to approach someone else on the street.

'Rosie don't!' Jake pulled his sister aside and sat her down.

'Where on earth are we, Jake?'

'I don't know, but I feel that the people of Drakemore may be under a curse. Don't speak to or approach any more people.'

They sat by a wall to watch the enigma, and an unusual tiredness came upon Jake. He yawned as if gulping in a barrelful of air. Tears flowed down the side of his cheek.

'Jake, are you okay?'

'I'm not sure. I feel rather tired and sluggish suddenly. I think I may need to rest.'

'But we've just rested!'

'I know, Rosie, but I feel tired. I can't feel my feet, either, and my hands are tingling. I don't know what's happening to me.'

Rosie grabbed some water from Jake's satchel and splashed it in his face. 'Wake up!' she shouted.

'I feel so tired, Rosie, I think – '

Rosie leaned over her brother and shook him. 'You think what, Jake?' she asked. 'You think what?'

Jake looked at Rosie. He tried to mouth something, but he was unable to sound out his words. His eyelids threatened to draw slowly down as if they were curtains. Then, like a puppet without someone to take hold of his strings, his head sunk to his chest.

He sensed nervousness overtaking Rosie, as he felt her sitting at his feet, clinging to his legs, but he was powerless to do anything about it. Through his semi-closed eyes, he saw her check out the passers-by, seemingly more afraid of their strange persona than before. She looked as if her feelings of loneliness had saturated her heart.

'Jake,' she whispered. 'Jake?'

Jake heard her, but he was powerless to respond.

'Oh, no, Jake. Please, don't do this to me.'

His body remained on the floor adjacent to an old white cobblestone wall. Jake was aware of Rosie on her knees beside him, her back facing the people. She looked quickly over her shoulder every time she heard footsteps on the sandy road.

Rosie sat there sobbing until something seemed to catch her attention. Jake heard hooves clonking against the rubble in the distance. He saw her look over to see a short, elderly man pulling a donkey. Rosie watched as the man moved towards them. He noticed that the man was wearing white linen trousers, a light brown top, and clean leather sandals. Although he looked to be a senior in appearance, he presented as being highly alert and certainly not as lost as the others they had encountered.

The man stopped in the distance and glanced at them before continuing to pull his donkey. As he approached them, Jake could see that he was smiling, and he had the presence of mind to recognise that it was the first smile he'd seen since their arrival.

The man seemed to beam with joy. He gestured with his arms and said, 'Greetings, children. Welcome to Drakemore! The village god has met you, I take it.'

Jake wanted to reply, but he could not. Rosie also remained silent.

'Now, now children, no need to be afraid. Be assured: you are in good company.' Jake perceived the man as he kneeled beside him and leaned in to examine him. 'Hmm...you look younger than I expected, but I do not doubt you are able. Leviathan told me that you would come one day, and truly, he is expecting you,' he whispered.

'Do you know where Leviathan is?' Rosie asked, having heard what the old man had said to her brother.

'Yes, but first, we must get your brother something to drink. Help me place him on my donkey, will you?'

Rosie cleared the croakiness in her voice and said, 'Yes. Sure.'

Jake felt the donkey's every movement as they walked to a light grey stone hut – the stranger's home – a short distance away.

'We have arrived,' the old man said. 'Please, help me dismount your brother – these old arms are not as youthful as they once were.' Jake detected a smile on the man's face as he watched through squinted eyes. He also felt pride in Rosie's maturity in caring for him.

Jake felt the two of them take him inside, his arms flung over their shoulders.

'Over here,' the old man said, directing them towards a long wooden ledge.

'Is he going to be all right?' Rosie asked. Jake felt her stroke his head.

'Yes, my dear, he will be just fine. Unfortunately, he was taken out by Hermes's sting.'

'Hermes's sting? What's that?'

'You weren't fortunate enough to encounter it yourself. It is said that when one greater than she arrives, she contests his arrival and prevents him from entering Drakemore. Your brother will be fine. He possesses great power, you know.'

He was aware of Rosie smiling and humbly agreeing. 'Yes, I know,' she said.

What were they talking about? Great power? What great power?

'Now, we just need to stir up some herbs, and he'll be as good as new.'

The old man took a pinch from the green leaves hanging from the low ceiling and placed it in the large clay cooking pot on the stove filled with boiling water. When he dipped his finger into the mixture to taste, Jake marvelled at how his finger did not burn.

'Hmm…just a pinch more basil,' he said, and he resumed his humming. He added more herbs and stirred the mixture a final time before pouring it into a large bowl, taking a wooden spoon, and serving the warm droplets to Jake. 'Just a drop or two should be sufficient.'

Jake felt his eyes twitch when he tasted the concoction, and he was soon able to fully open his eyes.

'Greetings, child,' the old man said as if in admiration of what was before him.

Rosie called his name and helped him to sit up. She squeezed him so tightly he could feel her bones pressing against him.

He felt his body, surprised that he was still alive. 'I thought I was dead.'

Rosie assured him in a whisper, 'This old man saved your life. He is for good and not for harm.'

'Thank you, sir,' Jake answered.

'You are most welcome. You can call me Maxwell.'

'Thank you, Maxwell.' Jake looked around the small room with its curved roof and asked, 'Where am I?'

Maxwell smiled and gestured to the room around him. 'My home. Welcome to my abode. Your arrival has been long-awaited. I'm so glad to finally meet you.'

'He knows Leviathan,' Rosie interjected.

'Really?' Jake sprung to his feet. 'Where is he? I must find him. We don't have much time left.'

'I will show you where he is, but I must warn you: facing Sebastian is no easy feat.'

'It is late, so you both can stay here for the night, and we shall set out in the morning.'

Rosie looked at Jake. Her round eyes shone like the sun reflecting off a tropical ocean, and she smiled. Her energy seemed to fill the room like the aroma of herbs on the stove.

Jake sighed. He sat back down and twiddled his fingers on the window ledge behind him as he watched the endless moonlit sky through the small glass window.

⟶ ❈ ⟵

'Ethan, please send for three black stallions.' Maxwell stood at the entrance to his stone hut and sent the instructions forth to a young boy who was standing with a long wooden stick, shaking cherries from the tree opposite his home. The boy dropped the stick and ran off to follow the orders. Jake watched Ethan's speed from the window and was intrigued to see a boy who looked his age working with such diligence.

It was early in the morning, and many people were working outside on various endeavours. Some built huts. Others sold food. Still others harvested crops. Everyone seemed to have work to do, although they did it slowly, and every movement seemed arduous. Ethan seemed to have more vigour than his counterparts.

Within minutes of Maxwell's request being sent, three horses came galloping around the corner, and the boy knocked on Maxwell's door. 'Sir, your horses are here.'

'Thank you, Ethan.' He took the few coins Maxwell offered him, ran back under the tree, and resumed working on collecting cherries for lunch, though his focus was now on the hut.

'Let's go now, children. Our horses await us outside!' said Maxwell to Rosie and Jake.

As the three sojourners left Maxwell's home, Ethan looked at Rosie as if he were stunned by her beauty. Rosie was so tired from having such little sleep that she barely noticed.

They all mounted their horses, and the three of them trotted off with Maxwell leading the way towards the village's tallest mountain.

→⁂←

They began to slow as they drew near the mountain. Though it was a picturesque day, the sun beat down on their brows. 'Let us water our horses now, for the mountain is very steep, and this heat will drain them of strength,' Maxwell instructed.

They dismounted, took their horses to the small stream for watering, and sat on the grass, watching them drink bountifully as the sun continued to shine on their faces.

'It's been a while since I've been this way. I had forgotten how scenic the journey was,' Maxwell said.

Rosie smiled and agreed. 'It is beautiful,' she said. 'You can hear the birds singing and see the butterflies flapping their delicate wings. The streams are glistening, and I have also spotted several rabbits, hopping in the fields.'

'You've seen nature at its very best, Rosie. How about you, Jake? What has this short journey been like for you?'

'I've been wondering why we're travelling up the mountain to see Leviathan, and why he is so far away from civilisation.'

'Hmm…that's an interesting observation. I see that you're a real thinker.'

Jake nodded.

'Well, if you must have the answers to your questions, I can tell you.'

Jake listened with his head bowed. He snapped strands of dry grass from their roots and kept them in his pocket to feed his horse on their travels.

'When they kept Leviathan behind during the Great Departure,' Maxwell began, 'they made sure to keep him at Hemferplin's highest point. They said he needed to reside there to ward off foreign invaders with his powers, but the truth was they were also fearful that someday, someone would come to rescue him.'

Jake felt slightly nervous, knowing that he would soon meet Sebastian who might potentially resist them. He wondered about Maxwell's relationship to the wise man, raised his head, and asked, 'How did you find him?'

'I am Hemferplin's chief messenger, and I would travel up there to pass on news from neighbouring precincts on occasion. Matters like trade prices and local battles are my main concerns. Anything else is handled by the Conteurs, but since the Great Departure, the climate of affairs in Drakemore gradually changed. When the seers left, something left with them. Foreigners no longer wanted to trade with us or be associated with our people. We became like a people cast-off; they called us the untouchables.'

'What was it they took?' Jake questioned.

'They took something which is intangible, to be honest. I've never quite been able to put my finger on it, but when you speak to Leviathan, he will say they took nothing when it is *we*, the people of Drakemore, who are cursed because we failed to see.'

'See what?' Jake asked.

'We failed to see that the gateway to the other world was through the seers.'

Jake went silent for a moment and then said, 'But it's not too late.'

'I know, child. I've always known that the decision to expel the seers was the worst that Drakemore has ever made, but the time I have spent with Leviathan has allowed me to realise there is a greater purpose at work. I believe your job here is important, Jake – you must commit yourself to it.'

'But I'm only twelve-years-old!'

'Do not say that. I have observed that your wisdom is beyond your years. You have an insight that I wish I possessed at your tender age. Your sister has it, too. You are two very special people.'

Jake and Rosie looked at each other, and he felt the strength of the bond between them, like an unspoken melody that had just been sung. He plucked up some more grass and fed his horse, stroking it as he thought upon what had been said. When he looked up at the mountain, he could sense that something revolutionary was about to happen there.

There were only two days before the blood moon, and Jake needed time to gather his thoughts. 'Would you both excuse me, please?' he asked.

'Yes. Sure, Jake,' Maxwell replied.

Jake walked into the fields and sat down in an array of yellow buttercups. He picked one, brought it up under his chin, and began to weep. 'I miss you, Grandpa,' he said. 'Just when I need you the most, you're not here. That mountain looks so treacherous, so frightening – I do hope to find the old man and help the people of Hemferplin, but it's such a tiresome task. Why did you leave me to do this without you? It's such a huge responsibility.'

He sobbed some more but then wiped his tears, determined not to let the others see him cry. As Jake dried his eyes, he felt an overwhelming sense of comfort, as if his grandpa had placed his hand upon his shoulder and said, 'I am with you.'

'I suppose I'd better go now. They'll be waiting on me.' Jake stood up, dusted himself off, and headed back towards Rosie and Maxwell, but when he looked in their direction from the field of flowers, he couldn't see them. Where were they?

Jake ran back to where he had left them, but they seemed to have vanished along with the three horses.

'Where have they gone?' Jake wondered out loud. 'Rosie!' he called.

Screams came from the mountain.

'No…no…noooo!' he shouted. His voice was so powerful a cry, animals in the area scattered, reacting in fright.

'Bring her back!' Jake said as he ran towards the mountain. 'Rosie, I'm coming to get you…Rosieeee!'

He could still hear his little sister's screams. Overtaken by emotion, emboldened to fight and defend, he began climbing the mountain.

CHAPTER EIGHT

The Mountain

The night closed in as Jake climbed in desperation to find his sister, though he could no longer hear her cries. Only the howls of the midnight owls echoed through the thick darkness.

Jake's legs trembled with every step. His hands were cold and bleeding, having been shaved on the sharp rocks which he could no longer see. He panted for air which felt scarcer the higher he climbed. Jake sought to find a path, which seemed an impossible task.

'Somebody help!' he cried.

He felt around for a level surface and fell backwards onto a small rocky plain. Flashing white dots emerged before his eyes. 'I can't do this,' he said. 'I've tried, but I can't. Rosie, please hold on, my sweet sister. I'm struggling to find you, but it's a struggle to breathe. It's also a struggle to fight.'

With this, his body shut down. Exhaustion had taken over, and whether he slept or fainted, he had no recollection.

—❧ ❦ ❧—

When the sun rose to full strength, Jake's eyes began to flicker. He felt something soft and furry on his face and recognised the smell of his lion's breath.

'Dux, you found me! How long was I sleeping?' Jake sat up slowly and caressed his companion. 'I've missed you.'

Dux growled softly and rubbed his weighty body against Jake's small frame.

Jake looked at Dux anxiously and asked, 'Have I missed it? Have I missed the blood moon?'

Dux growled gently again.

Jake thought he knew what the sound meant. He smiled through dry, cracked lips. 'Thank you for coming. I had no strength to continue. They've taken Rosie. We must get her back.'

Dux motioned his head sideways at a bag attached to his body.

'You've brought me food.' Jake smiled again and felt his eyes water. He sat upon the plain and ate his provisions: soft, sweet, warm bread, cured fish, multigrain seeds, and goat's milk.

When he was done, he looked into Dux's eyes and said, 'This is so energising. My father was right – a friend really does meet your needs when you need it most. Thank you so much, Dux.'

74

Jake smiled and took in a deep breath, moist with cold dew. He opened his satchel and pulled out the light-brown scroll along with a cotton bandage to wrap his wounds.

'Look,' Jake said, pointing to the tallest mountain on the map. 'The map I have would suggest we are here.' How he wished that Mount Gene would give up his sister. He would be more satisfied with that outcome than with the food Dux had brought.

'We must go, Dux. We don't have much time. We must find Leviathan and get Rosie back before the blood moon tonight. I need her by my side when I drink the potion.'

Dux began leading the way, motioning with his head for Jake to mount his back.

'I'm so glad you found me, Dux. I thought I was going to die there. The higher I climbed, the colder and more vicious the weather felt. It was my lungs – I could hardly breathe.'

Dux growled with a soft, authoritative tone. By then, Jake knew what each of his sounds meant. That growl meant that Dux had wanted Jake to talk less to conserve his energy.

Jake stood. He felt a sharp pain in his foot but ignored it, too bemused by the small raindrop that had made contact with the side of his cheek. Jake held up his hands towards the sky, and his arms were soon wet from the increased rainfall.

Dux looked up, too. The sun's rays had dispersed, stolen away by the grey clouds. There was a small whirlwind in the sky, seeming to gain force by the second.

The lion motioned for Jake to climb his back once more.

Jake attempted to do so, but he limped on his leg. 'My ankle feels sprained, Dux.'

Dux looked down at Jake's foot and then up at the whirlwind, which cut through the elements like a sharp blade. He looked down at Jake's foot again.

To Jake, it felt as if time had momentarily frozen, and his head seemed to spin in circles.

The black vultures chose that moment to fly towards them. There were three of them, black vultures with arms, legs, and round, glaring eyes like humans but with carnivorous teeth.

Dux growled viciously. With his mouth open and canines revealed, the lion lunged forward and bit into the human birds who fought back, digging their teeth into Dux's side, piercing his flesh.

'Dux!' Jake called. He stood there and cried uncontrollably, wanting to help but knowing there was nothing he could do.

'Get off him!'

The creature stopped and looked Jake in the eyes, tilting its head slightly.

Dux seemed to gather even more strength when he saw the sinister look in the creature's eyes. The lion flung it off and took a lethal bite into its skull, leaving no chance of survival. Other vultures screeched when they fell, wounded as they fought for their lives.

As it lay dying on the floor, the creature stared at Jake and dragged itself towards him like a lizard beating through the dust. It pointed its long, fungus-laden fingernails at him and ceased to be.

Jake's cries seemed to penetrate the isolated mountain as he stood and watched the onslaught. Dux turned towards him, his mouth bloody, and walked back slowly with his head down. Limping towards his friend, Jake wiped his eyes and hugged him. 'Thank you, Dux. You saved me.'

The whirlwind drew nearer. As if feeling the force of its reverberations, Dux suddenly leapt hundreds of feet up the mountain, almost as if the lion had flown. He looked down at Jake, but before the young warrior became anxious by their separation, a magnetic force catapulted him through the air, and he landed seamlessly on Dux's back.

'Wow! That was awesome.' Jake smiled.

Dux nodded and then leapt to the top of the mountain with great speed. Jake held on tightly, feeling the skin on his face being pushed back by the barbarous wind, and he imagined that his hair, usually curly, had lost every splendid ringlet. The force silenced him. It was so strong he struggled to open his eyes and breathe. Surrendering to its power, he pressed his head closely against Dux's wet fur and hoped the journey would be swift.

They arrived at the top of Mount Gene in less than a minute. Jake caught his breath and said, 'Oh, my, Dux – we are here.' He continued to hold tightly onto Dux as the sky opened with a torrential downpour. Jake shouted, 'I think we might need to find some shelter.'

Dux stood still, waiting as if he had heard or felt something.

'What is it, Dux?'

The elements had changed as though giving way to the arrival of the young soldier – the rain subsided within seconds, and the wind held back its tempest. The sun's rays appeared shyly from behind the sombre clouds seemingly ashamed by their initial departure and betrayal.

'Oh, look, Dux – it's a rainbow!'

Dux nodded his head.

Jake held out his arm. Shades of blue, purple, yellow, pink, and green reflected from his skin.

A butterfly landed on Dux's nostrils. He sneezed and scared it away.

Jake giggled. He dismounted from Dux, put weight on his injured ankle, and felt that it had strengthened. 'It seems like that wind did a world of good, Dux.'

Dux gave no response but to stand before Jake, waiting as a servant waits before his master.

'It feels rather calm up here, Dux,' Jake said, avoiding his friend's change in demeanour.

Dux remained silent.

Jake held onto Dux and knelt before him. 'Oh, I knew this time would come.'

Dux motioned his head towards the green pastures.

'I know you are always beside me, and I know you will never leave me. I thank you for all you have done,' Jake said, clearing his throat and sniffling.

Jake had clearly grown. Mount Gene had matured his soul, simply by the nature of its harsh and rocky existence. He drew closer to Dux and squeezed him a final time, then patted his back. 'Farewell, friend.'

Dux roared, walked to the edge of the awesome mountain, and flew off, vanishing into the other world, immersed in the multi-coloured rays of the rainbow's reflection.

Jake reached for his satchel, placed his map upon the grass, and wiped his wet eyes. Before him was an array of woodland, just as he had seen through the Magitheum. Thomas had left an old pocket sundial watch in a small, animal skin bag at the base of the satchel. He removed it, placed the dial upon the ground where it would catch the sun which had increased its shine, and waited for the shadow to cast.

There it was. The reality of the time caused his heart to skip a beat – there were only six hours left before midnight.

An urgency rushed through his bones like waves gushing upon the sea. 'Rosie!' he shouted. He collected his belongings and hurried off.

CHAPTER NINE

Leviathan

In Jake's view was a medium-sized house, surrounded by forest trees, the only one on the top of the mountain.

'Rosie!' Jake cried as he approached the house. The sound of his voice had deepened, echoing courage and valiance, but he still felt his heart race with the fear of the unknown. He drew nearer and heard what sounded like his sister calling his name. Jake put his ear to the wooden door and heard what seemed to be footsteps pacing a creaky wooden floor.

Jake looked through the letter slot to see a rugged old man with sweat dripping from his forehead.

'Right. I know what I'll do. I'll serve him some hot cocoa and cinnamon,' the old man said and appeared to look across the room at someone for approval.

'Haha! You must be out of your mind. *My* brother? Drink *your* cocoa and cinnamon? Haha.'

It was Rosie. Jake instantly recognised his sister's voice, but he could not see her. He listened further.

'Stop right now. You must stop your insinuations. 'Leviathan, tame her, won't you? She speaks as if one's suggestions are madness. Wait – are they madness? No, they are sure, very sure, aren't they, Leviathan? Very sure – tell her, Leviathan. I speak with confidence.'

Rosie was with Leviathan, but who was the old man?

Jake moved to the window in the direction the old man was facing, and he could see Leviathan and Rosie sitting behind a metal cage railing. Rosie's head was buried in her hands.

I must go inside, Jake thought. He knocked on the door so loudly the wooden structure seemed to shake.

When the door opened, the old man in dusty, ragged clothes brushed himself off, cleared his throat, and with a huge smile that revealed a mouthful of decaying brown teeth said, 'Good day. I'm much obliged. Please, do come in.'

Jake barged through the door, pushing the man aside, and he rushed to the cage. 'Rosie – '

'Jake!' Rosie's face beamed with sudden joy like a budding flower.

'Rosie, how do I get you out of there?'

'Sebastian has the key,' she replied.

'You mean that old man is *Sebastian*?

'Sebastian, you must open this cage right away!' Jake ordered.

'Now, there is nothing to worry about, child.' Sebastian pointed to an old wooden rocking chair in the corner opposite the prison and said, 'Please, take a seat, and I will explain this seemingly unscrupulous situation.'

Jake shook the railing forcibly. His arms were no longer lean, and small veins protruded from beneath his skin. He paused briefly and was drawn to Leviathan, who was watching him. Jake extended his hand through the bars and into the enclosed prison. 'You must be Leviathan.'

Leviathan received Jake's hand and pressed it against his cheek to convey warmth through the gates of his eyes, which were blurred with tears. The defences of his soul that he had built long ago seemed to open with a wave of gratitude. Each strand of his shiny white long hair seemed to speak a thousand words. His body suffered from malnutrition, confirming Erwin's concerns.

'Yes, it is I. Well done, son. Well done.'

Jake looked at Sebastian on his right, and he suddenly realised that Sebastian resembled Maxwell. 'Rosie, where is Maxwell?' he asked.

'Jake, meet your foe, *Max-well*. It's insane, I know.'

'Hold on – you mean Sebastian *is* Maxwell?' Jake studied the old man.

'Foe? Noooo, no, no, Jake – I am not a foe.' Sebastian bit his teeth together as his eyes moved skittishly around the room. The wealthy look Maxwell had once boasted drained from his appearance.

'What on earth happened to you, Maxwell? Your clothes are all torn, you smell like dried fish, and why did you take my sister?' Jake felt his face grow hot.

'Jake, he's under the curse,' Rosie shouted as she looked at Sebastian and shook her head. 'The moment we entered this dusty old, wasted house, he changed into this smelly...*thing*.' Rosie wiped the tears from her face.

The curse had affected Maxwell, too?

'But how did you manage to deceive us?' Jake questioned. 'You were so kind and helpful.'

'Jake, it's no use asking him anything; he's mad and unpredictable,' Rosie cautioned.

Sebastian sat on the rocking chair, swinging back and forth as though he was no longer present and his soul had left his body.

'Child, sit down, Sebastian will not harm you now, he has entered one of his trances and he will remain like this for at least one hour, so we do not have much time. I will explain that of which you are in search. I am certain we will be released from here, but first, there are some things which I must show you,' Leviathan said.

Jake recognised a fatherly look in Leviathan – it was the same look he'd seen in his grandpa and Thomas – and he sat with his legs crossed close to the prison bars.

Before, Leviathan was a young soul who had travelled long and hard, and whose heart was now desperate for answers he could not find on his own.

'My grandpa said you would know,' Jake began.

'Your grandfather has never erred from the truth, which is why he was chosen to be the keeper of records. Now, there are only a few hours before the blood moon, and it's important that you know the purpose for which you are now here. Now, are you ready?' Leviathan said with eyes that seemed able to peer into Jake's soul.

'Yes, I believe so,' was Jake's response.

Leviathan turned his back towards Jake, reached for the flask of water in the corner of his prison cell, and poured it on the floor. The water suddenly rose like a fountain and swirled unaided with great power. Inside the water, various colours began to form. They pieced together like a puzzle, and then figures appeared before them.

'Whaooo,' Rosie shouted as both siblings watched in amazement.

'What is *this*?' Jake exclaimed.

'This is my very own Magitheum.' Leviathan smiled. 'As the oldest standing seer, I have the privilege of seeing into the past. Please, look inside. There are some answers you have been looking for.'

'Who is *that* man?' Jake asked.

They watched as a man who looked to be in his early forties rushed around what looked like the historical streets of Drakemore, shouting, 'I had a dream that there is another world…and people…it is *so* beautiful!'

'That, children, is Godfrey-Jacob, the founding father of the seers' clan.'

'Who are those people he is speaking to?' Jake asked.

'Oh, those people? They were the village elders who sat on the Council.'

'I don't get it. He's so desperate to tell them about his dream.' Jake was

deeply intrigued.

'Yes, Jake. Desperate is an understatement. You see, he wanted them to prepare, for he was informed that a time would come when they would be able to cross over and experience the other world for themselves.'

Jake's eyes widened so far back that he felt his forehead crinkle slightly.

'But they're looking at him like he's mad,' Rosie noticed.

'Yes, sister – that is just what I was thinking, also,' Jake added.

'You are both right.' Leviathan confirmed. 'They thought he was highly irrational, a man who dabbled in witchery, but it was a good thing Godfrey was not deterred by their accusations.'

'What did he do?' Jake asked.

Leviathan blew with the force of a strong wind into the mysterious standing fountain.

Jake looked on with his eyes still widened. The scene had changed.

'What's he cooking?' Rosie asked.

Godfrey-Jacob was in a kitchen stirring a concoction over a hot stove. He added some ingredients, and it turned purple and bubbled over. 'An unknown messenger visited Godfrey in a dream,' Leviathan explained. 'He told him that the people of Hemferplin would not listen to his words and that their disobedience would, one day, cause them to be bound by their foolishness. He instructed Godfrey to prepare a potion which would contain all of their wicked endeavours and place it in a large bottle that one day, a great vessel would drink of its contents and reverse the curse intended for the people of the Hemferplinian Kingdom.'

'He listened to his inner-compass,' Jake thought aloud.

'Something I can see you have learned to do,' Leviathan said to Jake, smiling through his eyes.

Jake took a deep sigh and nodded.

'Wait – who is the woman?' Rosie asked.

'Oh, the woman who has just walked into the kitchen is Sharonai, Godfrey-Jacob's wife.'

'She is *so* beautiful.' Rosie complimented.

'Yes. She was from a tropical island where it was said that women were made from the finest of minerals on the seashore.' Leviathan laughed.

Jake felt inspired. 'It feels so special to know who we came from,' he whispered.

'I'm in love,' Rosie said. 'They are such a *beautiful* couple.'

Leviathan gazed out of the caged window to his right, observed the sky, and then blew upon the water fountain again. Suddenly, a young man appeared, sitting at a wooden table. He wrote upon a scroll with a feather dipped in black ink.

Jake squinted his eyes. Somehow the man's features looked familiar.

'Many years after Godfrey-Jacob and his wife had died, this young man with Godfrey's blood running through his veins purer than anyone had ever known decided to put a historical genealogical record together to seek out members of the authentic Godfredite tribe. By then, they had mixed with the locals and had their children. He began by summoning them one by one, exhorting them to return to the prescribed teachings of their forefathers.'

'Who is that man?' Rosie asked.

'I think I know, Rosie,' Jake interjected.

'The man you see there, dear children, is your beloved grandfather, Joe-Jacob Herlon, my dearest cousin.'

Jake smiled and sighed.

Leviathan lifted his trousers to withdraw a scroll from a cloth tied around his leg. He passed the scroll to Jake to open.

Jake unrolled the lengthy, beige-coloured scroll. 'Is this *that* scroll?' He pointed to the scroll upon which his grandpa was writing.

'Yes, Jake. That is the scroll of your entire lineage. The only ones missing from it are you and Rosie.'

Jake examined the scroll and said, 'This is incredible. Grandpa Joe achieved this?'

'He was the brightest and bravest I'd seen in our time, and I will tell you, I've seen many warlords, wizards, leaders, and rebels, but none like this one. He gathered seven thousand of us, but not all wanted to return. The seers' clan attracted great divisions. Houses were divided against houses, children against their parents, and parents against their children.' He paused for a moment, no doubt, to recall a memory of those times.

'Are you okay, Leviathan?' Rosie asked.

'Yes. I was just recounting some thoughts.'

'Were they good thoughts?' she probed.

'I was thinking about my mother. She was snatched from my father, Issachar-Jacob, at night while they were sleeping. Your Grandpa Joe, and I were together that night, as he had stayed with us. We could never forget what happened. We were small boys, but we always blamed ourselves for not fighting.'

'My grandpa saw it, too?'

'Yes, son. We both witnessed the horrific crime that left our family broken. That's why the timid were scared to follow, and these men were vicious.

We continued to proclaim the same warning of which Godfrey-Jacob had spoken, but as he said, the people would never heed our premonitions.

'Meanwhile, the potion became stronger and intensified due to their wicked endeavours. I watched the man you see before you slowly wither, hour by hour, day by day, year by year because he refused to let his people listen.'

Rosie looked at Sebastian, who was sat in the corner still rocking back and forth on the chair with his eyes rolled to the back of his head. Rosie shook her head.

Leviathan wiped his face with his handkerchief and said, 'We worried about Joe's memory after he decided to move to Reeva to protect his family because he travelled across the Illunaus. The sting of the sea spirits always affects the mind. When the seers learned that he had been preparing his grandchild, it gave us all hope that his mind had not been completely fragmented by the sea spirits.'

'What do you mean? I never noticed. His mind was completely normal. In fact, he had an excellent mind,' Jake stated.

'Yes, Grandpa was sharp,' Rosie affirmed.

'Indeed, your grandfather's mind was excellent. He was like a master craftsman, which is why he was able to retain his most important memories after crossing the Illunaus, but you must understand that it wasn't complete.' Leviathan wiped his eyes.

'Now, children – please do me the honours. Take this pen and write your names on the bottom of the scroll. I have waited a long time for this moment.'

'Sure,' they both answered. They wrote as neatly as they possibly could.

CHAPTER TEN

Reunion

'Wait – you people speak of the *Purple Potion*?' Sebastian said, as one whose mind had just returned from an out of body experience.

'Yes, the Purple Potion,' the three of them replied simultaneously.

'But if you drink the potion, you will die. No one has tasted it and survived.'

'Do you know where it is?' Jake asked.

'Yes. I've been keeping it for years.' Sebastian resumed rocking on the chair.

Leviathan's voice turned stern as if he were speaking to an untrained animal. 'The boy is here for the potion, Sebastian. Give the boy what he has come for and release the girl.'

'P…powers. Give me your powerrrsss,' Sebastian said to Jake.

'But I don't have any powers.'

'Trouble not the boy, Sebastian. He has nothing to give you.'

Sebastian wagged his long, bent finger at Jake and moved slowly towards him. 'So, how did you get here? You deceive yourself – you have come from the other world, haven't you?'

'No, I am from Reeva, a small village near the Hill of Pikascia.'

'Open these prison doors now, Sebastian!' Rosie demanded.

'Sebastian, let the girl go – she is of no use to you – and give the boy the potion. The power you have been searching for all these years does not exist.'

'What about all the people *you* have warded off, Leviathan? If you could deter the foreign invaders, then this young vessel who the gods claim is stronger can surely have a whole nation bowing at my knees. Isn't that right, little soul?'

Jake was unable to find the words to respond.

'You see, Jake, I have been waiting a very long time for your arrival. Leviathan said there is one who is greater en route. Now that you are here, how could you think I would release you so soon?' With that, Sebastian's body grew to seven feet tall. His skin thickened, he grew scales like a crocodile, and he stood on all fours.

'Jake, watch out,' Rosie shouted.

Two heads like iguanas formed, one at either end of the creature's body, and a horn protruded from each of its crowns.

'There is another way to find the path you seek, Sebastian, but you must seek it with a *pure* heart,' Leviathan told him. 'This is not the answer!'

'What's happening, Leviathan?' Jake stepped away from the creature; his body felt as if it were moving underwater.

'It's the potion, Jake. It's absorbing the fullness of Sebastian's wickedness,' Leviathan answered.

'I have long told you that it cannot be taken by force or manipulation, Sebastian. Now, let the boy do what he came to do.'

Sebastian roared. Fire came from his mouth.

Jake ducked and dodged the flame but narrowly so.

'Jake!' Rosie shouted.

Just then, a sword and shield appeared in Jake's hands.

The lizard-like creature moved towards Jake, breathing out fire. Jake resisted the flames with his shield. Balls of fire bounced of his weapon and flew back towards the creature.

'Jake, get him!' Rosie cried.

Jake looked at Rosie and then at Leviathan. Rosie was holding on to Leviathan's arm through the metal bars separating them, and they were both on the floor, seeking cover from the flames.

Unsure of what to do, Jake charged towards the creature and pierced the sword through its arm. The sword was so sharp and the strength used so great, that it penetrated through the wall of the house, pinning the creature to the corner like a restricted prisoner. Green blood seeped from the creature's flesh. Sebastian groaned in pain, his power and flames slowly diminished.

Jake quickly took several steps backwards. As he moved, he stepped onto a wooden plank, caught his foot and tripped over. Light from beneath the floor crept around the broken plank.

'Child, that's the potion! The Purple Potion is down there! Go down and drink it,' Leviathan instructed. His thin body lay on the floor with Rosie, their hair and skin dripping wet with sweat from the heat of the flames.

Jake grabbed another plank beneath him and pulled as hard he could; it came away.

Sebastian roared desperately trying to unpin himself from the wall. Blood oozed everywhere.

'Quick!' shouted Rosie with a mixture of authority and panic.

'We haven't got much time', said Leviathan shielding himself from Sebastian's angry roars of fire.

Hurriedly, Jake pulled up other planks until there was enough room for him to climb down. 'I'm going down,' he said as he climbed through the small gap in the floor to slide on ropes like liana vines; it was a jungle. It looked and smelled like it was from the other world.

The potion sat there on a wooden chest of drawers, glowing with full purple brilliance, as though its colour was more defined than what he knew could possibly be real. The floor had patches of grass on it that seemed to have fought for growth through the rotten wood.

Jake's lower body felt weak as he approached the antique bottle, embossed with gold. Something, which felt like fire, bubbled within him. It was surreal yet deeply personal.

He realised there was no time left and that he had to drink the potion, and then his lips touched the rim of the bottle, and its contents trickled down his throat like a waterfall cascading over a ledge.

The ground shook, pushing Jake to his knees. He looked at his body and saw the potion radiating through his skin. He felt a current flow like a stream, through every fibre of his being, from head to toe.

Jake heard a loud clang like the sound of the metal cage door flinging open.

'We're free,' Rosie shouted.

Rosie and Leviathan climbed down the ropes to meet Jake.

Barely able to move or speak, Jake remained on his knees with his arms wide open in a position of surrender.

'When will it stop?' Rosie asked, observing her brother as he was overtaken by the powerful current.

'As soon as the panther, Erwin, and Thomas arrive,' Leviathan replied.

Rosie waited silently on her knees, watching her brother. Jake could see in her eyes that she wished to embrace him, but the power of the purple current appeared to keep her away.

Rosie looked out of the basement window in front of them and said, 'Leviathan, look.'

'It's the blood moon,' Leviathan confirmed.

'The sky is orange, Jake, and the moon is red. You did it, Jake. You drank the potion before the blood moon,' Rosie said excitedly.

Jake slowly closed and opened his eyes. He felt a strong feeling of relief, and a tear rolled down his cheek from his left eye.

Leviathan fixed his eyes towards the sky. 'Well done, Jake, but there's more.' With those words, the ground shook again, so mightily this time, it caused them all to fall on their backs.

Jake heard Leviathan gasp as if air were filling his lungs. Still unable to rise, he turned to look at him and witnessed Leviathan transform into a young man. His skin was no longer wrinkled but tender and youthful. Leviathan slowly stood to his feet, a handsome, muscular man with short black ringlets and golden-brown complexion.

'No way, Leviathan!' Rosie jumped up and danced. 'You look great, Leviathan!'

Jake smiled with his eyes when he saw Leviathan's cheeks blush.

Within moments, Erwin and Thomas came through the forestry walls. They had also become youthful and very handsome. The panther followed behind them.

'Leviathan!' the brothers shouted as they ran towards him to form an embrace.

The panther, chief keeper and king of the other world, strode towards Jake. He examined his body with his yellow eyes and put his paw on the centre of his forehead. The current left Jake and flowed into the black, silky-skinned wild cat. Before them, the panther stood on its hind feet and metamorphosed into a tall, hazel-skinned king. He was wearing a golden crown, a blue linen royal robe embellished with precious rubies and diamonds around the hem, and holding a golden sceptre in his right hand.

Now able to move, Jake pushed himself away from the royal figure. No one uttered any words; it was a solemn moment.

The king motioned with his hand to Erwin who removed a parcel wrapped in a black velvet cloth from his large satchel. Inside was a golden crown, slightly smaller than the king's, embellished with various jewels of purple, red, green, and blue. 'Please, come and receive your honour.' His tone was soft and comforting to Jake's ears.

'You are going to make Jake a *prince*?' Rosie asked.

'Your brother has always been a prince. It is only now that he is mature enough to receive his crown. Having overcome every form of wickedness that would try to prevent you from fulfilling your purpose, Jake, it is now time to be crowned the prince you have always been.'

Jake moved towards the king, then paused. 'Wait – there is something I must do.'

The king looked at Jake as if he knew his intention.

Jake climbed up the ropes to the floor above with his muscular arms and agile legs. Before him slithered a black and green snake. Jake thought this must be what Sebastian was now reduced to.

'You, Sebastian, you have hurt so many people by preventing them from knowing the truth. Your greed and evil have brought you to this place where all you will do is move on your belly and eat the dust on the ground forever!' Jake pointed to the door and said, 'Now, go, Sebastian, and never return!'

The snake slid through the gap in the door.

Jake wondered where those words had come from. It was as if they had been on his tongue, waiting to be released all along. At that moment, he felt one with the wisdom of the seers. He took what he felt to be a final look around the room and climbed back down to receive his crown. They all applauded the soon-crowned prince as he returned, and he felt a sense of pride fill his soul.

'You, Jake, have done what no one else could do because nobody's heart was as pure, sincere, and courageous as yours.' As the royal figure spoke, the walls extended, and the grass fully matured on the ground.

Leviathan, Erwin, and Thomas stood side by side, beaming with energetic excitement as they looked at the mature young man.

'You have merged the two worlds together. The people of Hemferplin have been chosen to enter the other world to see it in all its glory and lead the nations, but they have struggled due to their callousness of heart, and their wicked leader, Sebastian,' the king continued. 'But you were appointed to destroy the curse which held the people back and free them from its power. So now, you are honoured with a position of royalty in the new world.'

Jake smiled as the crown was placed on his head.

Rosie ran to hug him. 'You're royalty, Jake.' She laughed.

'I guess that makes you royalty, too, my sister,' Jake said. He winked at Rosie, and she gave him a cheeky smile in return.

Jake could no longer see where the walls ended, and the forest began. Beautiful tropical trees of green, glistening streams, and birds singing in the sun-filled sky surrounded them.

Rosie smiled as she spun around, her arms wide open as if taking in all its beauty.

Jake looked at his sister and smiled. Again, no words could articulate what they were seeing or feeling.

'Please, follow me,' the king instructed. They walked over ground laden with pure white sand. 'You will remember Jezrel,' the king said to Jake.

'Mr Jezrel, yes, of course. My grandfather – '

'Pleased to meet you,' interrupted a tall, muscular man. He bowed his head full of black ringlets and shook Jake's hand.

'Jezrel was the first seer to receive an official warning from the elders of the Council,' the king explained.

'Good-day, Jezrel,' the brothers greeted and bowed their heads.

They walked further, their bodies soaking up the sun.

'This is Henknel, Pentrick, and Jockneu,' the king continued.

Before them stood what appeared to be a row of warriors wearing linen shorts, their chests revealed. They were all tall and muscular and bore scars on their flesh, which Jake discerned could only have been the result of ferocious battles.

'These were some of our bravest warriors who fought for the survival of the seers' clan,' the king explained. 'You would have seen some of their weaponry on your way to the other world, and indeed, *in* the other world.'

'Yes,' Jake recalled. He felt honoured to have met them. He wondered why he had been introduced to only Henknel, Pentrick, and Jockneu when behind them stood what looked to be an array of many more warriors.

The king seemed to have perceived his thoughts and said, 'You will surely grow to learn and understand the order of warriorship.' The king gave Jake a warm smile.

Jake smiled back, understanding that he was in the company of the highest order of warriors.

As they continued to walk, they came across a young girl with long brown shiny hair, wearing a long white silk dress embellished with a blue ribbon, drawing water from a well. She turned and waved at them with a pleasant smile as they approached.

The king stopped near her and looked as if he were filled with compassion. 'Rosie, meet Lacey,' the king said.

Rosie smiled, waved back, and said, 'Pleased to meet you.'

Jake waved, too, and said, 'Nice to meet you, Lacey.'

They stopped and stared at each other for a brief moment, then continued to walk.

'You will remember Lacey from the village when you first arrived,' the king said.

Rosie's eyes widened. She covered her mouth and whispered, 'The lifeless girl?'

'Yes. You see, Rosie, life has a strange way of teaching us that friendships can be found in the least expected places.'

Rosie looked back to see Lacey waving goodbye. She waved back with a smile, and they continued their walk through the merged worlds, the king revealing hidden secrets on the way.

Lightning Source UK Ltd.
Milton Keynes UK
UKHW021151090921
390255UK00002B/141